Merlin and the Dragons

Merlin and the Dragons

JANE YOLEN

ILLUSTRATED BY

LI MING

PUFFIN BOOKS

To Christopher McKerrow, he knows why.
—J.Y.

To Joshua M. Greene, for his friendship,
guidance, and encouragement.
—L.M.

PUFFIN BOOKS
Published by the Penguin Group
Penguin Putnam Inc., 375 Hudson Street, New York, New York 10014, U.S.A.
Penguin Books Ltd, 27 Wrights Lane, London W8 5TZ, England
Penguin Books Australia Ltd, Ringwood, Victoria, Australia
Penguin Books Canada Ltd, 10 Alcorn Avenue, Toronto, Ontario, Canada M4V 3B2
Penguin Books (N.Z.) Ltd, 182-190 Wairau Road, Auckland 10, New Zealand

Penguin Books Ltd, Registered Offices: Harmondsworth, Middlesex, England

First published in the United States of America by Cobblehill Books,
an affiliate of Dutton Children's Books, a division of Penguin Books USA Inc., 1995
Published in Puffin Books, 1998

21 23 25 27 29 30 28 26 24 22

THE LIBRARY OF CONGRESS HAS CATALOGED THE COBBLEHILL EDITION AS FOLLOWS:
Yolen, Jane.
Merlin and the dragons / by Jane Yolen ; illustrated by Li Ming.
p. cm.
Summary: When young Arthur is troubled by dreams, Merlin tells him a story about a fatherless boy
who himself dreamed about dragons and the defeat of the evil king Vortigern.
ISBN 0-525-65214-0
1. Arthur, King—Juvenile fiction. 2. Merlin (Legendary character)—Juvenile fiction.
[1. Arthur, King—Fiction. 2. Merlin (Legendary character)—Fiction.] I. Li Ming, ill. II. Title.
PZ7.Y78Md 1995 [Fic]—dc20 94-46861 CIP AC

Puffin Books ISBN 978-0-14055891-3

Manufactured in China

Illustration concept by Iain McCraig, animator, illustrator, screenwriter, and filmmaker.

A NOTE FROM THE AUTHOR

UTHER PENDRAGON took the crown of England by force in terribly troubled times. Worried that his newborn son, Arthur, might be in danger, he gave the infant to his court magician, Merlin, for safekeeping. Merlin took the baby to the faithful Sir Ector and at Ector's far-off estates the child grew up never knowing who his real father was.

Uther died without revealing that he had an heir, but Merlin caused a sword to be magically embedded in stone bearing the legend: "Who pulleth out this sword from this stone is rightful king of all England." Many men seeking to become king tried to pull the sword out, but they all failed.

One day young Arthur, acting as his foster brother's squire, was sent home from a tournament to find his brother's lost sword. Coming upon the stone, and without reading the words, he pulled the sword out as easily as if it had been set in butter. So he became king of England, though he felt himself a fraud. Only was it later revealed by Merlin that Arthur was the son of Uther and at last the boy believed himself worthy of reigning as king.

Arthur gathered about him knights pledged to do noble deeds and when they were in Camelot—Arthur's great castle—they sat at the famous Round Table which—legend tells us—could seat 150 knights.

T HE NIGHT was dark and storm clouds marched along the sky. Rain beat against the gray castle walls. Inside, in a bedroom hung with tapestries, the young King Arthur had trouble sleeping. Awake, he was frightened. Asleep, he had disturbing dreams.

At last he climbed out of bed, took a candle to light his way, and started out the door. Suddenly remembering his crown, he turned back and found it under the bed where he'd tossed it angrily hours before. It felt too heavy for his head, so he carried it, letting it swing from his fingers.

As he walked along the hall, strange shadows danced before him. But none were as frightening as the shadows in his dreams.

He climbed the tower stairs slowly, biting his lip. When he reached the top, he pushed open the wooden door. The old magician was asleep in his chair, but woke at once, his eyes quick as a hawk's.

"What is it, boy?" the old man asked. "What brings you here at this hour?"

"I am the king," Arthur said, but softly as if he were not really sure. "I go where I will." He put the crown on Merlin's desk.

"You are a boy," Merlin replied, "and boys should be in their beds asleep."

Arthur sighed. "I could not sleep," he said. "I had bad dreams."

"Ah . . ." Merlin nodded knowingly. "Dreams." He held out a hand to the boy, but Arthur didn't dare touch those long, gnarled fingers. "Let me read your dreams."

"It is one dream, actually," Arthur said. "And always the same: a fatherless boy who becomes king simply by pulling a sword from a stone."

"Ah . . ." Merlin said again, withdrawing his fingers. "I know the very child. But if you cannot tell me more of your dream, I shall have to tell you one of mine. After all, a dream told is a story. What better than a story on a rainy night?"

Arthur settled onto a low stool and gazed up at the wizard. A story! He hadn't known he wanted a story. He'd come seeking comfort and companionship. A story was better than both.

He listened as Merlin began.

In a small village high up in the rugged mountains of Wales lived a lonely, fatherless boy named Emrys. Dark-haired he was, and small, with sharp bright eyes, and a mouth that rarely smiled. He was troubled by dreams, sleeping and waking. Dreams of dragons, dreams of stone.

His mother was the daughter of the local king and tried to be both mother and father to him. But a princess is only taught lute songs and needlework and prayers. She'd never once climbed a tree after a bird's egg or skinned her knee pursuing a lizard, or caught a butterfly in a net. Emrys had to invent that part of growing up himself. And a lonely inventing it turned out to be.

The other boys in the village teased him for not knowing who his father was. "Mother's babe," they cried, chasing him from their games.

So Emrys went after birds' eggs and lizards, butterflies and frogs by himself, giving them names both odd and admiring, like "flutterby" and "wriggletail," and making up stories of their creation. And he chanted strange-sounding spells because he liked the sounds, spells that sometimes seemed to work, most times did not.

But he never told his dreams aloud. Dreams of dragons, dreams of stone.

Now in the village lived an old man who knew all sorts of things, from reading and writing to how birds speak and why leaves turn brown in autumn. And because Emrys was the son of a princess, the grandson of a king, the old man taught him all he knew.

It was this learning that brought the village boys to him, not in friendship but in curiosity. They would ask Emrys to show them some trick with the birds, or to tell them stories. Glad for the company, Emrys always obliged. He even took to making up harmless predictions to amuse them.

"The rain will soon fall," he would say. And often it did.

"The first spring robin will arrive." And soon after, it came.

Now any farmer's son could have made the same right guesses and after awhile the village boys were no longer impressed. However, one day Emrys found a book of seasons and planetary movements in the old man's cottage and read it cover to cover. Then he went out and announced to the astonished boys: "Tomorrow the sun will disappear."

The next day at noon, just as the calendar had foretold, an eclipse plunged the countryside into darkness. The boys and their parents were equally horrified and blamed Emrys. From then on he was called "demon's son" and avoided altogether.

Years went by and Emrys grew up, terribly alone, dreaming dreams he did not understand: dreams of a shaking tower, dreams of fighting dragons.

One day when Emrys was twelve, a cruel and ruthless man named Vortigern came to the valley. Vortigern had unjustly declared himself High King over all Britain. But the country was at last in revolt against him and he had been forced to flee, riding ever farther north and west. At last he had arrived at the foot of Dinys Emrys, the mountain which towered above the village, with a bedraggled army on tired horses, bearing tattered banners emblazoned with red dragons. A handful of court magicians rode with them.

Vortigern pointed to the jagged mountain peak. "There," he said in a voice hard and determined. "There I will build my battle tower, so that I may see my enemies when they approach."

He turned to his soldiers. "Gather the people of this village and bring them to me, for they will be the hackers and haulers. They will make me a tower of stone.'"

Young Emrys looked on in amazement. Banners sewn with red dragons? A tower of stone? Such things had been in his dreams. What could it all mean?

The Welsh stonecutters began their work under the watchful eyes of the soldiers. For many days they mined the stone, cutting huge pieces from the sides of Dinys Emrys. They swore they could hear the cries of the mountain at each cut.

Next they hauled the stones with ropes, their little Welsh ponies groaning with the effort. Finally, came the day when they built the tower up on the mountainside, stone upon stone, until it rose high above the valley.

That night Emrys went to bed and dreamed once again his strange dreams. He dreamed that the tower—the very one built by Vortigern—shook and swayed and tumbled to the ground. And he dreamed that beneath the tower slept two dragons, one red as Vortigern's banners, and one white.

That very night the High King's tower began to shudder and shake and, with a mighty crash, came tumbling down. In the morning, when he saw what had happened, Vortigern was furious, convinced the villagers had done it on purpose.

"Your work is worthless," he bellowed at the Welshmen. "You will be whipped, and then you will get to work all over again."

So the Welshmen had to go back to their stonework, great welts on their backs. They hacked and hauled, and once again the tower rose high above the valley. But the night they were finished, it was the same. The tower shook and tumbled to the ground. By morning there was only a jumble of stones.

Vortigern drove the villagers even harder, and by the following week the tower was once again rebuilt. But a third time, in the night, a great shudder went through the mountain and the work once again lay in ruins. Vortigern's rage could not be contained. He called for his magicians. "There is some dark Welsh magic here. Find out the cause. My tower must stand."

Now these magicians had neither knowledge nor skill, but in their fear of Vortigern they put on a good show. They consulted the trees, both bark and root; they threw the magic sticks of prophecy; they played with the sacred stones of fate. At last they reported their findings.

"You must find a fatherless child," they said. "A child spawned by a demon. You must sprinkle his blood on the stones. Only then will the gods of this land let the stones stand." They smiled at one another and at Vortigern, smiles of those sure that what they ask cannot be done.

Vortigern did not notice their smiles. "Go find me such a child."

The magicians stopped smiling and looked nervous. "We do not know if any such child exists," they said. "We do not know if your tower can stand."

Furious, Vortigern turned to his soldiers. "Gold to whomever brings me such a child," he roared.

Before the soldiers could move, a small voice cried out. "Please, sir, we of the village know such a boy." The speaker was a spindly lad named Gwillam.

"Come here, child," said Vortigern. "Name him."

Gwillam did not dare get too close to the High King. "His name is Emrys, sir. He was spawned by a demon. He can cry the sun from the sky."

Vortigern turned to the captain of his guards. "Bring this demon's son to me."

At that very moment, Emrys was on the mountain with the old man, absorbed in a very strange dream. Under the ruins of the tower he saw two huge stone eggs breathing in and out. Just as he emerged from his dream, he was set upon by Vortigern's soldiers. "What shall I do?" he cried.

The old man put a hand on his shoulder. "Trust your dreams."

The soldiers quickly bound Emrys and carried him to the High King, but Emrys refused to show any fear. "You are the boy without a father, the boy spawned by a devil?" Vortigern asked.

"I am a boy without a father, true," Emrys said. "But I am no demon's son. You have been listening to the words of frightened children."

The villagers and soldiers gasped at his impudence, but Vortigern said, "I will have your blood either way."

"Better that you have my dream," Emrys said. "Only my dream can guide you so that your tower will stand."

The boy spoke with such conviction, Vortigern hesitated.

"I have dreamed that beneath your tower lies a pool of water that must be drained. In the mud you will find two hollow stones. In each stone is a sleeping dragon. It is the breath of each sleeping dragon that shakes the earth and makes the tower fall. Kill the dragons and your tower will stand."

Vortigern turned to his chief magician. "Can this be true?"

The chief magician stroked his chin. "Dreams <u>can</u> come true . . ."

Vortigern hesitated no longer. "Untie the boy, but watch him," he said to his soldiers. "And you—Welshmen—do as the boy says. Dig beneath the rubble."

So the Welshmen removed the stones and dug down until they came to a vast pool of water. Then the soldiers drained the pool. And just as Emrys had prophesied, at the pool's bottom lay two great stones. The stones seemed to be breathing in and out, and at each breath the mud around them trembled.

"Stonecutters," cried Vortigern, "break open the stones!"

Two men with mighty hammers descended into the pit and began to pound upon the stones.

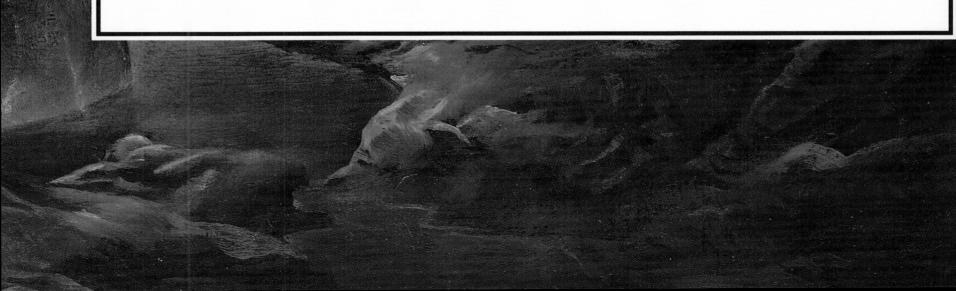

Once, twice, three times their hammers rang out. On the third try, like jets of lightning, cracks ran around each stone and they broke apart as if they had been giant eggs. Out of one emerged a dragon white as new milk. Out of the other a dragon red as old wine.

Astonished at the power of his dreaming, Emrys opened and closed his mouth, but could not speak. The men in the pit scrambled for safety.

The High King Vortigern looked pleased. "Kill them! Kill the dragons!"

But even as he spoke, the dragons shook out their wings and leaped into the sky.

"They are leaving!" cried the chief magician.

"They are away!" cried the soldiers.

"They will not go quite yet," whispered Emrys.

No sooner had he spoken than the dragons wheeled about in the sky to face one another, claws out, belching flame. Their battle cries like nails on slate echoed in the air.

Advancing on one another, the dragons clashed, breast to breast, raining teeth and scales on the ground. For hour after hour they fought, filling the air with smoke.

First the red dragon seemed to be winning, then the white. First one drew blood, then the other. At last, with a furious slash of its jaws, the white dragon caught the red by the throat. There was a moment of silence, and then the red dragon tumbled end over end until it hit the ground.

The white dragon followed it down, straddling its fallen foe and screaming victory into the air with a voice like thunder.

"Kill it! Kill the white now!" shouted Vortigern.

As if freed from a spell, his soldiers readied their weapons. But before a single arrow could fly, the white dragon leaped back into the air and was gone, winging over the highest peak.

"Just so the red dragon of Vortigern shall be defeated," Emrys said, but not so loud the High King could hear.

Cursing the fleeing dragon, Vortigern ordered the tower to be built again. Then he turned to Emrys. "If the tower does not stand this time, I *will* have your blood."

That night young Emrys stared out his window, past the newly built tower. A hawk circled lazily in the sky. Suddenly the hawk swooped down, landing on his window ledge. There was a moment of silent communion between them, as if Emrys could read the hawk's thoughts, as if the hawk could read his. Then away the hawk flew.

Mountains, valleys, hillsides, forests gave way beneath the hawk's wings until, far off in the distance, it spied thousands of flickering lights coming up from the south. As if in a dream, Emrys saw these things, too.

Emerging from his vision, Emrys turned from the window and went downstairs. He found King Vortigern by the foot of the tower.

"I have seen in a vision that your fate is linked with the red dragon's," Emrys cried. "You will be attacked by thousands of soldiers under the white dragon's flag—attacked and slain."

Vortigern drew his sword, angry enough to kill the boy for such insolence. But at that very moment, a lookout atop the tower shouted:

"Soldiers, my lord! Thousands of them!"

Vortigern raced to the top of the tower stairs and stared across the valley. It was true. And as he watched further, one of the knights leading the army urged his horse forward and raced along to the tower foot, shouting: "Come and meet your fate, murderous Vortigern!"

Vortigern turned to his own men. "Defend me! Defend my tower!"

But when they saw the numbers against them, the men all deserted.

"Surrender, Vortigern!" cried a thousand voices.

"Never!" he called back. "Never!"

The old wizard stopped speaking.

"Well?" Arthur asked. "What happened to Vortigern? You cannot end a story there."

Merlin looked at him carefully. "What do *you* think happened?"

"Vortigern was slain, just as Emrys said."

"Is that the boy speaking?" asked the wizard. "Or the king?"

"The boy," admitted Arthur. "A king should forgive his enemies and make them his chiefest friends. You taught me that, Merlin. But what did happen?"

"The men of the white dragon defeated Vortigern all right. Burned him up in his own tower."

"And that knight, the one who rode up to the tower first. What became of him?"

"His name was Uther Pendragon and he eventually became the High King," Merlin said.

"Uther," mused Arthur. "He was the last High King before me. But then he was a hero. He was fit to rule. Perhaps one of his sons will come to claim my throne."

"Uther had only one son," Merlin said softly, "though only I knew of it." He looked steadily at the boy. "That son was you, Arthur."

"Me?" For a moment Arthur's voice squeaked. "Uther was my father? Then I am not fatherless? Then I am king by right and not just because I pulled a sword from a stone."

Merlin shook his head. "Don't underestimate your real strength in pulling that sword," Merlin cautioned. "It took a true and worthy king to do what you did."

Arthur gave a deep sigh. "Why did you not tell me this before?"

The old wizard's hawk eyes opened wide. "I could not tell you until you were ready. There are rules for prophets, just as there are rules for kings."

"So now I am king in truth."

Merlin smiled. "You were always king in truth. Only you doubted it. So you can thank your dreams for waking you up."

"What of Emrys?" Arthur asked. "What happened to him?"

"Oh—he's still around," replied the wizard. "Went on dreaming. Made a career of it." He rummaged around in some old boxes and crates by the desk until he found what he was looking for. "I still have this. Saved it all this time." He tossed a large yellowed dragon's tooth across to Arthur.

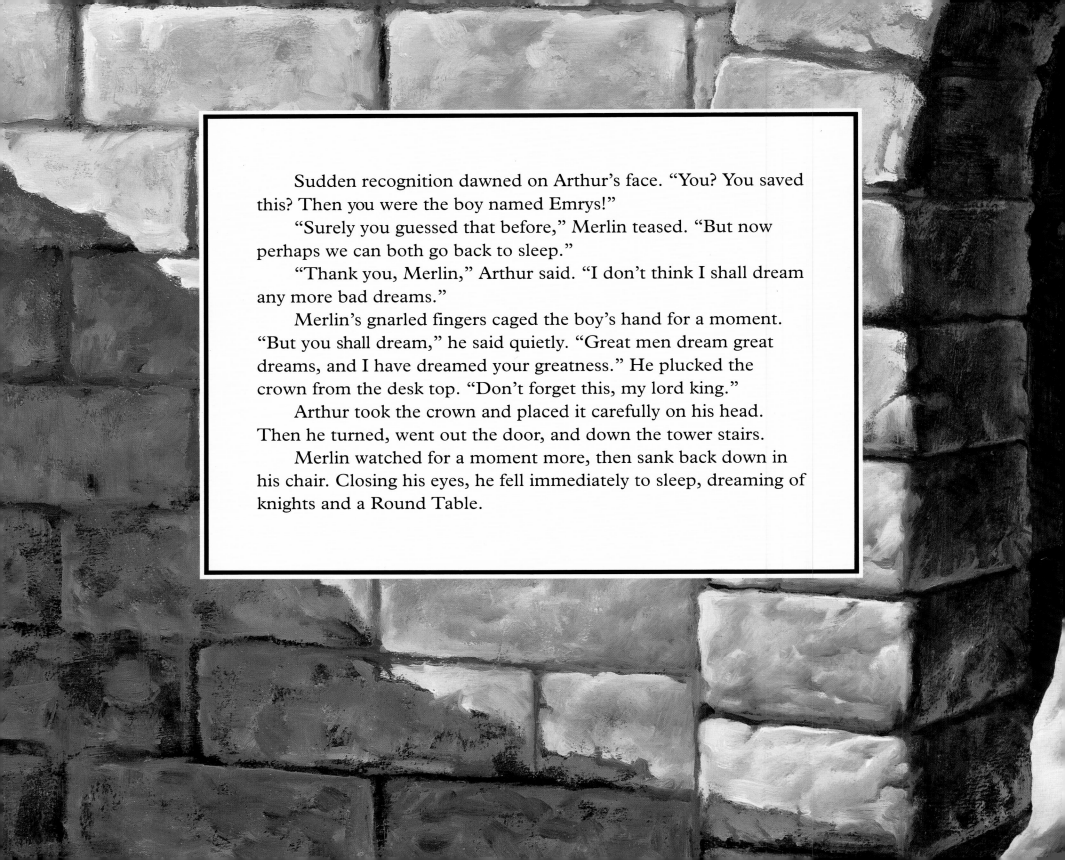

Sudden recognition dawned on Arthur's face. "You? You saved this? Then you were the boy named Emrys!"

"Surely you guessed that before," Merlin teased. "But now perhaps we can both go back to sleep."

"Thank you, Merlin," Arthur said. "I don't think I shall dream any more bad dreams."

Merlin's gnarled fingers caged the boy's hand for a moment. "But you shall dream," he said quietly. "Great men dream great dreams, and I have dreamed your greatness." He plucked the crown from the desk top. "Don't forget this, my lord king."

Arthur took the crown and placed it carefully on his head. Then he turned, went out the door, and down the tower stairs.

Merlin watched for a moment more, then sank back down in his chair. Closing his eyes, he fell immediately to sleep, dreaming of knights and a Round Table.

THE AUTHOR

Jane Yolen is the author of more than 150 books, including the Caldecott Medal–winning *Owl Moon*. Her fascination with King Arthur has led her to do a number of books about him, including *Merlin's Booke* and *The Dragon's Boy*, as well as a trilogy of novels about the young Merlin, *Passager*, *Hobby*, and *Merlin*. A past president of the Science Fiction and Fantasy Writers of America and a board member of the Society of Children's Book Writers and Illustrators for more than twenty years, she is also editor-in-chief of Jane Yolen Books, an imprint of Harcourt Brace Company. She lives in western Massachusetts and Scotland with her husband.

THE ILLUSTRATOR

Li Ming was born and raised in Shanghai, China. He spent five years as an artist at the Shanghai Animation Film Studio before immigrating to the United States in 1993. He is married and lives in New York City. *Merlin and the Dragons* is his first picture book.

Merlin and the Dragons is available on audiocassette,
compact disc, and animated video from Lightyear Entertainment,
350 Fifth Avenue, Suite 5101, New York, New York 10118
Call 1-800-229-7867 for information